MUFFIN MOUSE'S
NEW HOUSE

Written and illustrated by
Larry DiFiori

A GOLDEN BOOK • NEW YORK

Western Publishing Company, Inc., Racine, Wisconsin 53404

Muffin Mouse was in her house, drinking strawberry tea, when her friend Frankie Frog came by. "Do you want to come out to play?" he asked.

"It's too windy," said Muffin. "And it's starting to rain."

"That's OK with me," said Frankie. "I love to play in the rain."

"I don't like wind or rain!" said Muffin. "I'm staying inside where it's warm and dry."

Muffin shut her window tight. Then she made herself another cup of strawberry tea and started reading her favorite book when . . .

SPLASH! SPLASH! SPLASH! Water came dripping from the ceiling.

"There must be a leak in the roof!" cried Muffin.

WHOOSH! WHOOSH! WHOOSH! went the wind. The windows rattled and the house began to shake. Muffin ran outside to see what was happening.

CRASH! BANG! SMASH! Muffin Mouse's house came tumbling down.

"Oh, my poor house!" cried Muffin.

Frankie came running over. "Are you OK, Muffin?"

"I'm OK, but look at my house!" said Muffin.

"Don't worry," said Frankie, "I'll help you build a new one."

"It will take too long," answered Muffin. "I'm going to get one that is already made. And I know who might have one. Pack Rat Pete!"

Frankie went along with Muffin. They ran down a grassy hill and up a slippery slope.

On top of the slope was Pack Rat Pete's place. He collected everything.

"Hi, Muffin. Hi, Frankie. What can I do for you?" asked Pete.

"The wind knocked my house down," said Muffin. "I need a new one."

"Maybe you could use this," said Pete. He pointed to an old milk carton.

"You could cut out windows and a door," said Frankie.

Muffin shook her head. "No. No. It's much too small."

"Well, how about this big wooden box?" said Pete.
"But it's too plain," said Muffin.

"Wait. I have just the perfect thing," said Pete.
It was an old yellow rubber boot.

"You'll always stay dry in there," said Frankie.

"No. No. It's not right," said Muffin. "It wobbles too
much."

"I've got it!" shouted Pete. "How about this pretty blue bottle?"

"No. No," said Muffin. "Everyone could see inside."

Pete finally said, "I can't think of anything else you could use for a house, Muffin. But I can make you some strawberry tea. I'll put the teapot on."

"Tea! Teapot! That's it!" yelled Frankie. "Why didn't I think of it before? There is a broken teapot in the weeds near my house."

"As much as I like to drink strawberry tea, a broken teapot for a house doesn't sound too good," said Muffin. "Come take a look," pleaded Frankie.

So after thanking Pete for all his trouble, they ran down
the slippery slope and up the grassy hill.

They found the teapot not far from Frankie's house. Muffin ran over to get a closer look. She patted the shiny, smooth surface. She peeked inside. "Yes, yes, it's big enough and strong enough," she said.

"And it's very pretty, too," added Frankie.

Muffin and Frankie set to work right away cleaning and fixing the old teapot. Then after they moved Muffin's belongings over from her old house, Muffin made herself a pot of strawberry tea.

"Thanks to you, Frankie, I now have a fine new house. No rain will get in and no wind will ever knock it down," said Muffin.

Indeed, no wind ever did blow it down.

On rainy days Muffin stayed inside her house. And when she heard SPLASH! SPLASH! SPLASH! she knew it wasn't her roof leaking. She knew it was just her friend Frankie Frog playing in the rain.